Molly Mischief

Saves the World!

DEAN

Originally published in Great Britain 2018 by Pavilion Children's Books
This edition published 2023 by Dean, part of Farshore
An imprint of HarperCollins*Publishers*
1 London Bridge Street, London SE1 9GF
www.farshore.co.uk

HarperCollins*Publishers*
Macken House, 39/40 Mayor Street Upper,
Dublin 1, D01 C9W8, Ireland

ISBN 978 0 0086 1742 4
Printed in China
001

This book is produced from independently certified FSC™ paper
to ensure responsible forest management.

For more information visit: www.harpercollins.co.uk/green

Molly Mischief

Saves the World!

Adam Hargreaves

Hello, my name is **Molly.**
Most of the time I'm happy – happy making mischief.

That's why I'm called **Molly Mischief!**

But some things make me unhappy. Things like chores.

I don't like tidying my room.
But when I *do* tidy my room, Mum's not happy!

There's no pleasing her.

MOLLY!

I don't like unpacking the groceries.

But when I *do* unpack the groceries, Dad's not happy.

There's no pleasing him!

MOLLY!

And I don't like washing up.
But when I *do* the washing up, my brother's not happy.

Sometimes there's no pleasing anyone!

MOLLY!

I wish I could do all my chores in supersonic time.
I wish I had superpowers.
I wish I could be a superhero.

So I went upstairs and got dressed as...

SUPER-MOLLY!

I tidied my bedroom in super-quick time.

I vacuumed,

SUPER-MOLLY!

and polished,

SUPER-MOLLY!

put away the dishes,
SUPER-MOLLY!

mopped, **SUPER-MOLLY!**

and took out the rubbish. ALL in the blink of an eye!

I had *lots* of superpowers.

I was very **STRONG.**

I had **LASER EYES.**

I could walk on the ceiling.

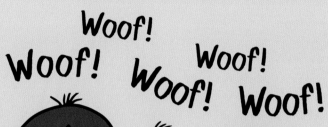

I could talk to animals.

I could leap over

TALL

buildings in
a single bound!

And I could fly!

Up! Up! Up!
And away!

I could fly my kite,
even when there was no wind!

And you ought to have seen me on my bike!

It was great fun having lots of superpowers.

It was also very useful.
It was useful when the bully at school tried to take my lunch money.

And it was useful when we got stuck in a traffic jam.

I helped an old lady cross the road, at *super speed.*

And then I realised I could be a real-life superhero.

I rescued a **whale** at the seaside!

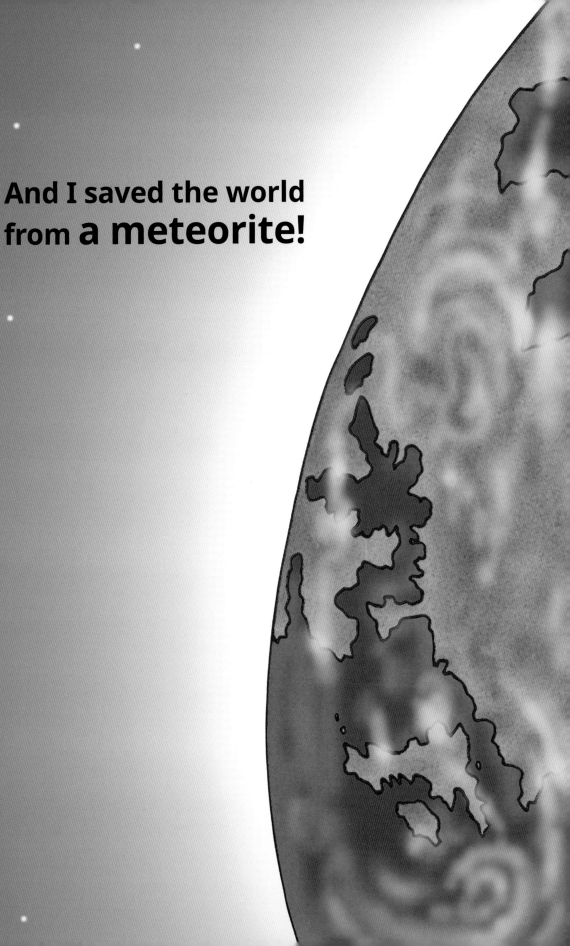

And I saved the world
from **a meteorite!**

Super-Molly became super-famous.
She was on the front page of the paper and starred on the TV news.

Daily News
Super-Molly saves the
World!

But nobody knew it was me.
Nobody knew all the good deeds I was doing.
It's no fun being famous and not being recognised.
It's no fun being good and not getting praise.

Being a superhero was also hard work.
I had to get up in the middle of the night to fight crime.

I had to miss my favourite dinner to capture an escaped lion.

And cleaning up the flood was no fun at all.

In fact, being a superhero was just one long list of chores!

So, I gave up being Super-Molly.

I decided it was much easier to do what I'm told.
Well, most of the time.

I *have* kept one superpower.
One superpower I would never give up.
I am super...

...Mischievous!